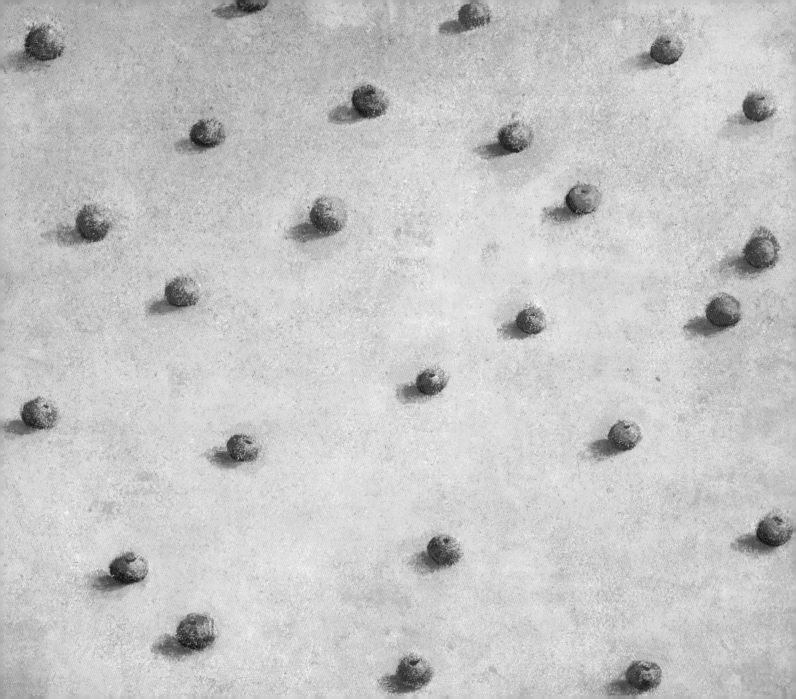

Javier Sáez Castán

The Three Hedgehogs

A pantomime in two acts and a colophon

DOUGLAS & McINTYRE   *A Groundwood Book*   **TORONTO VANCOUVER BERKELEY**

DRAMATIS PERSONAE

Hedgehog One

Hedgehog Two

Hedgehog Three

The Crow

The Farm Woman

The Cook and the Posse

The Apple Tree

The action takes place in the French countryside.

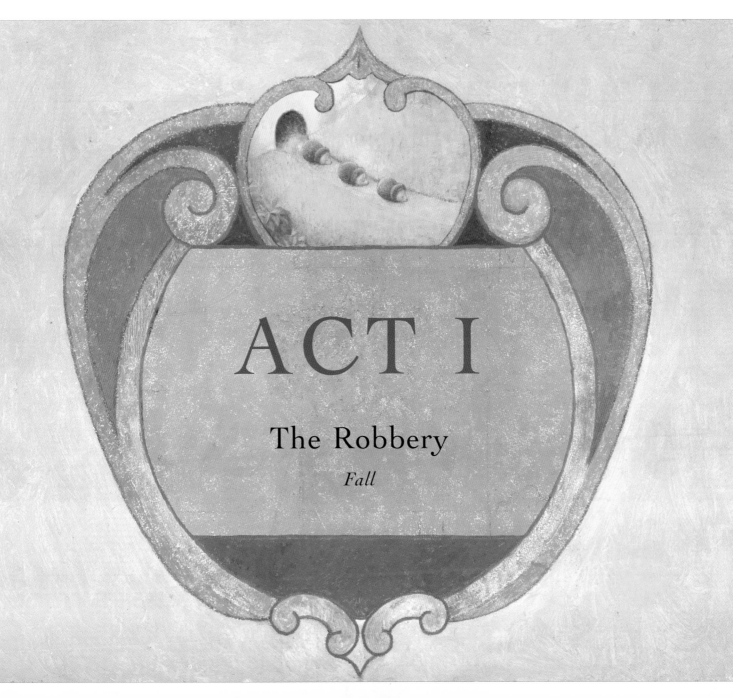

ACT I

The Robbery

Fall

Early one beautiful morning, three hedgehogs
leave their house to look for food.

They find a hole in a hedge and, lo and behold,
they walk through it into an orchard!

The hedgehogs tumble and roll among the apples,
and the apples stick to their spines.

"This is pure robbery!" screams the crow,
as the hedgehogs amble back through the hedge.

The three hedgehogs go home, thinking about
all those apples spread out on their tablecloth.

They eat every single one—so delicious—
and then they fall fast asleep.

"My apples! I've been robbed!" shouts the farm woman
in her orchard.

She rings a bell, and a posse sets out to find the thieves.
Meanwhile, the hedgehogs are snoring gently.

But the thieves are nowhere to be seen,
and they have left no tracks.

So the posse decides to go home. After all, winter is coming.
But in the spring, the culprits will pay the price.

ACT II

The Trial

Spring

In the spring, the posse sets off again,
determined to catch the thieves this time.

The three hedgehogs have woken up, and
they are warming their tiny snouts in the sun.

"There they are! Those three
are the guilty ones."

"They are trapped," croaks the crow.
"Don't shoot!" plead the hedgehogs.

"Lower your guns," cries the farm woman.
"Look over there, at the meadow. Isn't that an apple tree?"

"*It was the hedgehogs who planted me,*" says the apple tree.
"*Why would you kill them?*"

"They're the ones who threw away a few seeds when they had their delicious feast. And when the March showers came, I was born, in this garden."

The posse drops its weapons in shame,
and the hedgehogs make music at their feet.

Hands are held out in peace
as the heroes are honored for their good deed.

And as the day ends, the three hedgehogs
celebrate by dancing in the twilight.

COLOPHON

The Meal

The Next Fall

GLOSSARY

Pantomime: Normally there is no talking in a pantomime, but in this case, pantomime means a short, comic play.

Colophon: Normally a colophon is a note at the end of a book describing how the book was made. But in this case, the colophon is a short scene at the end of the play.

Dramatis Personae (Latin): A list of the characters in a play.

Tout pour la pomme (French): All for the apple.

Salve (Latin): A greeting.

Coupables de culpabilité (French): Guilty of being guilty.

Quitapenas (Spanish): Suspended sentence.

La pomme sur tout (French): The apple above all else.

Ericii me severunt atque eos necabitis? (Latin): The hedgehogs saved me and you are going to kill them?

Parvula semina nam iacuerunt (Latin): For now the tiny seeds lie on the ground.

Lautum ut suum convivium egerunt (Latin): They acted in order to clean up their feast.

Nata sum martiis imbribus primis (Latin): I was born in the first rainstorms of March.

Malus in hortis (Latin): Apple tree in the garden.

No tienen culpa (Spanish): Not guilty.

Los 3 erizos (Spanish): The three hedgehogs.

Paix (French): Peace.

Virtus omnia vincit (Latin): Virtue triumphs over all.

幸免 **Hsien mien** (Chinese): To escape by a hair's breadth.

安人 **An jen** (Chinese): To pacify the people.

Bon appétit (French): Enjoy your food.

Cuique suum (Latin): To each his own.

Note: The hedgehogs sometimes make mistakes in Latin.

Edited by María Cecilia Silva-Díaz
Art Direction: Irene Savino
Translations from the Latin: David Wachsmuth

Groundwood Books / Douglas & McIntyre
720 Bathurst Street, Suite 500, Toronto, Ontario M5S 2R4

Distributed in the USA by Publishers Group West
1700 Fourth Street, Berkeley, CA 94710

We acknowledge for their financial support of our publishing program the Government of Ontario through the Ontario Media Development Corporation's Ontario Book Initiative.

National Library of Canada Cataloguing in Publication
Sáez Castán, Javier
The three hedgehogs / by Javier Sáez Castán
ISBN 0-88899-595-4
1. Title.
PZ7.S13Th 2004   j863'.7   C2003-906306-2

Printed and bound in China by Everbest Printing Co. Ltd.

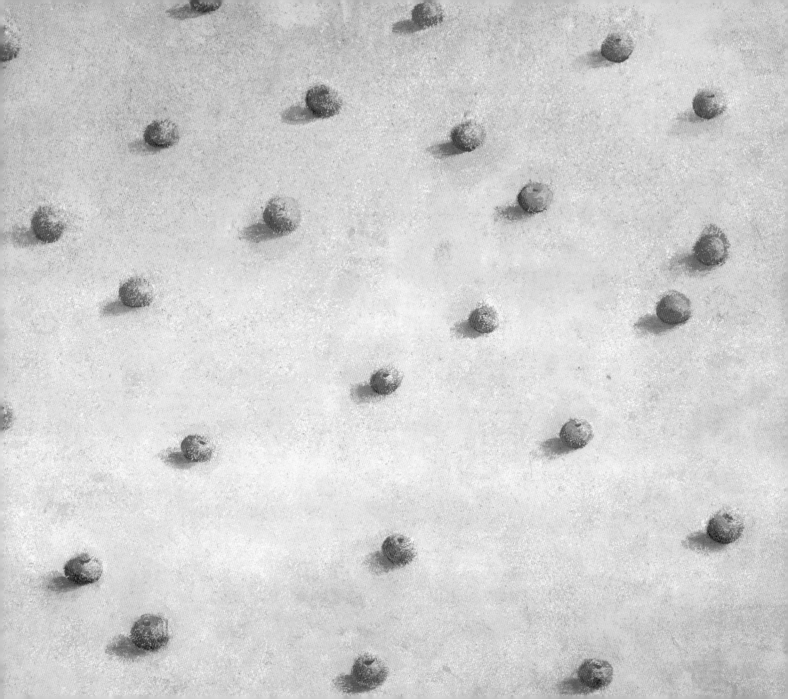